S0-AHR-654

Jim Arnosky

Rabbits & Raindrops

PUFFIN BOOKS

PORTER COUNTY LIBRARY

Valparaiso Public Library
103 Jefferson Street
Valparaiso, IN 46383

JJ FIC ARN   VAL
Arnosky, Jim.
Rabbits and raindrops /
33410011251370   AUG 2 3 2011

PUFFIN BOOKS
Published by the Penguin Group
Penguin Putnam Books for Young Readers, 345 Hudson Street, New York, New York 10014, U.S.A.
Penguin Books Ltd, 27 Wrights Lane, London W8 5TZ, England
Penguin Books Australia Ltd, Ringwood, Victoria, Australia
Penguin Books Canada Ltd, 10 Alcorn Avenue, Toronto, Ontario, Canada M4V 3B2
Penguin Books (N.Z.) Ltd, 182-190 Wairau Road, Auckland 10, New Zealand

Penguin Books Ltd, Registered Offices: Harmondsworth, Middlesex, England

First published in the United States of America by G. P. Putnam's Sons, a division of The Putnam & Grosset Group, 1997
Published by Puffin Books, a member of Penguin Putnam Books for Young Readers, 2000

15 17 19 20 18 16

Copyright © Jim Arnosky, 1997
All rights reserved

THE LIBRARY OF CONGRESS HAS CATALOGED THE G .P. PUTNAM'S SONS EDITION AS FOLLOWS:
Arnosky, Jim. Rabbits and raindrops / Jim Arnosky. p. cm.
Summary: Mother rabbit's five babies hop out of her nest to nibble clover, meet grasshoppers,
spiders, and bees, play tag, and run for shelter when it rains.
[1. Rabbits—Fiction.] I. Title.
PZ7.A7384Rad 1997 [E]—dc20 95-22921 CIP AC
ISBN 0-399-22635-4

This edition ISBN 0-698-11815-4

Printed in the United States of America
Set in Horley Old Style

Except in the United States of America, this book is sold subject to the condition that it shall not, by way of trade or otherwise,
be lent, re-sold, hired out, or otherwise circulated without the publisher's prior consent in any form of binding or cover other than
that in which it is published and without a similar condition including this condition being imposed on the subsequent purchase.

This book is dedicated to
Darren.

Mother rabbit sits
by her nest

under a hedge
at the edge
of green lawn.

Her five babies are ready
to climb out of the nest
for the first time.

Mother rabbit hops out
into the bright sunlight,

onto the green grass.

One after another,
the five baby rabbits
hop out onto the lawn.

They nibble clover
blossoms and leaves.

They meet grasshoppers,
spiders, and bees.

All of a sudden
the sky turns dark,
and big, heavy raindrops
begin to fall.

A rabbit's fur is not waterproof.
Baby rabbits can become
soaked, and catch cold.

So Mother rabbit hurries her
babies back under the hedge.

From their dry shelter,
five baby rabbits
watch the rain pouring down.

A butterfly flutters in
under the hedge,
and rests on a dry leaf.

Soon others come inside,
out of the rain.

Out in the shower, honeybees buzz by,

flying between raindrops to stay dry.

Suddenly the shower ends,

and the last few raindrops splatter down.

All together, the rabbits hop
out onto the lawn . . .

. . . to taste the wet grass,
and play rabbit tag
in the sun.